# Teddy
## in
# Trouble

# Teddy
### in
# Trouble

by Holly Webb

Illustrated by Sophy Williams

**tiger tales**

## tiger tales

5 River Road, Suite 128, Wilton, CT 06897
Published in the United States 2017
Originally published in Great Britain 2008
as *Timmy in Trouble* by the Little Tiger Group
Text copyright © 2008 Holly Webb
Illustrations copyright © 2008 Sophy Williams
ISBN-13: 978-1-68010-411-0
ISBN-10: 1-68010-411-X
Printed in China
STP/1800/0129/0317
10 9 8 7 6 5 4 3 2 1

For more insight and activities, visit us at www.tigertalesbooks.com

# Contents

For Eddie and Jamie — keep writing!

## Chapter One
# Katy's Christmas Wish

"How's yours coming along, Katy?" Dad asked.

"I'm just thinking...." Katy doodled in the corner of her Christmas present list. A little dog's face, with big long ears and round, dark eyes. She smiled to herself. He was cute!

"Well, it's only four weeks until Christmas," Dad pointed out. "Both of your grandmothers want to know what to get you as well, you know. You'll end up with socks if you don't give them some ideas."

Katy's list wasn't very long. Just a couple of books, some new sneakers, and a cell phone, which she knew she wouldn't get because her mom thought she was too young.

"Is that all?" her dad asked in surprise, looking over her shoulder.

Katy looked at him thoughtfully. Was now the right time to ask?

Dad glanced over at Diana's list. Katy's older sister was sitting on the other side of the table, and her list was enormous. It was also very messy. "I can't read any of that!" he complained. "You'll have to copy it over, Diana."

Diana looked down at her paper and grinned. "It's not my fault. Misty kept coming and sitting on it. You know what she's like! I had to write around her."

Misty the cat stopped washing her paws when she heard her name, and looked at them all innocently. *Who, me?* she seemed to be saying. She adored pieces of paper, and if anyone was writing, or reading a newspaper, she was never happy until she was sitting right in the middle of the page.

Diana leaned across the table to look at Katy's list, too. "You're not getting a phone," she pointed out. "Mom won't even let me have one. You can't only want a pair of sneakers."

"Sounds like a nice easy Christmas shopping trip," Mom said, coming into the kitchen.

Katy smiled hopefully. She'd only put the phone on the list so her parents would say no, and then hopefully they'd be more likely to say yes to what she *really* wanted. "So I can't have a phone, then?" she sighed.

"Absolutely not!" her mom said.

"Oh," Katy said, crossing it out. She tried to sound disappointed, but it wasn't very convincing. "Well, there is one other thing...."

Her dad folded his arms, smiling at her. "I knew it! Go on, break it to me gently, Katy. What is it, an elephant?"

Katy smiled back. "Not quite. But … it is an animal." She took a deep breath. "I really, really want a pet."

Mom and Dad exchanged a thoughtful glance, and Diana stopped chewing her pen and bolted upright.

"A pet! We can't have another cat! What about Misty? She'd hate it."

Katy shook her head. "I know. I don't want a cat. I want a dog. A puppy. That's what I'd absolutely, definitely, more-than-anything like for Christmas. Please?" she added, smiling as sweetly as she could at her dad. She knew how much he loved dogs….

"I'm not sure it's a very good idea,

Katy," Mom said slowly. She looked at Misty, who'd gone back to washing herself. "Diana, please don't let Misty sit on the table. Her paws are dirty."

"They can't be! She spends all day washing them!" Diana pointed out. "Anyway, she'll just jump up again when you aren't looking, Mom."

Mom picked Misty up and tickled her under the chin. "Not on the table, Misty," she said firmly.

Misty stared at her, waiting until she turned around. Then she leaped straight back up again. Katy, Dad, and Diana giggled, and Mom peered over her shoulder and sighed. "I think I'll just pretend I didn't see that," she muttered.

"Mom, why isn't it a good idea?" Katy asked pleadingly. "It would be wonderful to have a dog. You can train dogs," she added persuasively. "I'm sure a dog would be better behaved than Misty!"

Misty glared at Katy, then jumped onto Diana's lap. "Misty's very well behaved," Diana protested, petting her gently.

"Anyway," Diana continued, "I don't think Misty would like us having a dog. She hates dogs. Remember how upset she got when Jade from next door got under the fence? She hid at the top of the apple tree for hours!"

Mom nodded. "I know. Misty might not like it. We'd have to make an extra big deal over her. And who would take care of this dog when the two of you were at school? Me, I suppose!" But she was smiling.

"Well, if we did get a puppy, we'd certainly have to be careful. We'd have to introduce the puppy to Misty slowly, so they got used to each other." Dad smiled thoughtfully. "I had a dog when I was your age. It was a lot of fun— we went on walks together, in the park and down to the woods. And now that you're eight, Katy, I think you're old enough to help care for a puppy, feeding it and grooming it. Having an animal to take care of would help you to be more responsible."

"You mean we *can* have a puppy?" Katy cried, jumping up excitedly and almost knocking her chair over.

"No," Dad said firmly. "I mean we'll think about it. Not no, but not yes. We need to think it through very carefully. It's not something you can just decide in a moment."

But Katy had seen the wistful look in Dad's eyes when he was remembering those walks with his dog. And she was almost sure that really he meant yes.

## Chapter Two
# The Best News

Dad refused to say anything else about dogs that weekend. Katy tried asking a couple of times if he and Mom had had time to think about it yet, but she didn't want to get on his nerves right now. She couldn't believe that they actually might be getting a puppy! She'd hoped, of course, but hadn't really expected them to say yes, or even half-yes. It was so exciting!

She spent a long time on Sunday afternoon looking at her favorite dog websites on the computer, wondering what kind of puppy they might be able to get, and reading all the advice for new dog owners. There was an awful lot to learn. Especially if you already had another pet, like Misty.

Katy dreamed of dogs that night. She was running through the woods with a beautiful puppy, just like Dad had described. When she woke up, she had a huge smile on her face, although she couldn't quite remember what the puppy had looked like. *Brown and white*, she thought vaguely, *with big, floppy ears*. But she could remember his happy, excited little bark, and the soft feel of his springy fur under her hand. It was a wonderful dream. And it might, just possibly, be about to come true!

She was still smiling as she wandered downstairs for breakfast, with her school uniform on all crooked and her curly hair still full of tangles.

Mom took one look and sent her back upstairs. "Brush your hair, Katy, for goodness' sake. And put it in ponytails, because you have PE today." She smiled. "I'd hurry up if I were you. Dad and I have something to tell you both!"

Katy raced back up to the bathroom. As she galloped up the stairs, she could hear Diana asking what was going on.

Less than two minutes later, Katy was back. Her hair was in ponytails, although the ponytail holders didn't match, and one side was higher than the other. "What is it? What do you want to tell us?" she gasped as she dashed into the kitchen.

Dad chewed a mouthful of cereal very, very slowly, and winked. He was obviously enjoying keeping them in suspense.

Mom shook her head. "Don't tease Katy, Ken! It isn't fair!" She gave Diana a slightly anxious look as she said it.

"Okay, okay!" Dad put down his cereal bowl, and beamed at Katy. "Yes."

"Yes? Really?" Katy jumped up and down excitedly and ran to hug her dad. "When? This Christmas? We're getting a puppy for Christmas!"

"But you can't!" Diana cried. She pushed her plate away and stood up. "You just can't, Dad! What about Misty? Katy can't take care of a dog, anyway! And what about all those ads on TV about not giving dogs as presents? *A dog is for life, not just for Christmas.* All those poor puppies get abandoned every year! It's wrong!"

Dad nodded seriously. "I know, Diana. Sit down. You too, Katy. I haven't finished explaining."

Diana sat down, looking worried, and Katy sat, too, although she was so happy that she could hardly keep still.

Dad leaned toward them. "We're not giving you a puppy for Christmas, Katy—"

Katy's eyes opened wide with horror.

"But you said…."

"We are getting a puppy, but he or she will be a family dog. Like Misty is a family cat, Diana. You're right that Katy is a little too young to have all the responsibility of a dog by herself." Dad smiled at Katy. "There's a lot to do to take care of a puppy, so don't worry; there'll still be plenty for you to do."

Katy felt like cutting in and saying that actually, she was sure she *was* old enough, but she decided it was best not to.

Mom leaned over to touch Diana's hand. "Try not to worry, Diana. We know we're going to need to be really careful when Misty meets the puppy. We'll all do our best to make sure she doesn't get upset."

"And the puppy won't arrive at Christmas, Katy," Dad added. "We're going to try and get one before Christmas, if we can, or maybe afterward. Christmas is just too busy— it's not a good time to bring a new dog into the house. Mom and I have agreed that we'll look around for someone with puppies for sale locally. Happy now?" Dad beamed.

Katy nodded blissfully, but Diana was staring at the table, twisting her fingers together. "I still think Misty's going to hate it," she muttered. She looked anxiously over at Misty, napping by the kitchen radiator on her favorite pink blanket. It had been Diana's when she was little, and Misty had adopted it.

"What kind of dog should we get?"

Katy asked, ignoring her grumpy older sister. She wished she could remember the puppy in her dream better.

"Nothing too big!" Mom said quickly.

"But not too small, either. We want to be able to go on some good long walks." Dad sounded as though he was really looking forward to it. "Maybe a terrier? They're great dogs, really friendly."

"I've always liked pugs," Mom said thoughtfully.

"The ones with the squished-up faces?" Katy asked, giggling.

Mom nodded. "I like the way their tails curl up," she said, smiling. "What about you, Katy? This was your idea. What kind of dog would you like?"

Katy thought back to her dream. "What kind of dog has long ears?" she asked, wrinkling her nose as she tried to remember more. "A brown and white puppy with long ears. I dreamed about one like that last night."

Diana sniffed, as though she thought that was silly. "You can't get a dog because of a dream."

"Why not?" Mom asked gently. "Katy's been thinking about it a lot, Diana. That's probably why she dreamed about a puppy."

"Maybe it was a spaniel?" Dad suggested. He got up and disappeared into the living room. They could hear him muttering to himself as he searched the bookcase, and he came back with Katy's dog sticker book. "Was he anything like this, Katy?"

Katy took the book and gasped with

delight. There he was! A little brown and white dog, staring impishly out of the page at her, his eyes bright and alert. "A cocker spaniel," she muttered, reading the caption. "Oh, yes! I mean, I'd love any dog—even one with a squished face, Mom! But I'd really, really love one of those…."

## Chapter Three
# Puppy Playtime

A couple of days later, Katy was kneeling on the window seat in the living room, waiting for her dad to come home from work. As soon as she saw him walking down the street, she shot out of the front door and raced toward him.

"Hurry up, Dad! You're so late! I've been waiting forever!"

Her dad looked at his watch. "It's only

six o'clock, Katy. That's my usual time. Did your mom make a special dinner or something? What's the rush?"

"Oh, well, it feels later," Katy said excitedly. "We have to have dinner really quickly—we're going to see some cocker spaniel puppies! Mom found out about them, and the breeder only lives 20 minutes away!"

Luckily, Dad was as excited as she was, especially when he heard that Katy had seen pictures of the puppies on the breeder's website, and one of them was brown and white, exactly like the one in Katy's book. They both finished dinner long before Mom and Diana, and Katy glared at Mom when she started making a cup of coffee afterward.

"Mo-om!" she wailed. "We have to

go! We said we'd be there by now!"

Diana was still slowly finishing her yogurt, making each spoonful last, and Katy scowled at her, too. "You're doing that on purpose!" she said accusingly. "You don't even like yogurt all that much!"

"Go and put your coat on, Katy," Mom said. "We're obviously not going to get any peace until we go! Hurry up, Diana. You really are taking a long time."

Diana huffed but put the yogurt container in the garbage and went to get her coat, too. She looked like she was about to have a spelling test, not going to see a litter of beautiful puppies.

"What's the matter?" Katy asked her in the back seat of the car. She was so excited about seeing the puppies, but Diana was sending out a black cloud of gloom right next to her. Katy couldn't ignore it. "Are you jealous?" she whispered. "You're being so grumpy."

Diana looked like she might snap back, but then she sighed. "No. I'm just worried about Misty, that's all."

"She might like having a dog to make friends with," Katy suggested hopefully.

But Diana looked doubtful. "We'll see," she muttered.

The puppies were just as beautiful as Katy had imagined they would be. The breeder's house had a sunroom in the back, which was being used as a puppy room. Katy could hear the puppies squeaking and yapping as soon as they got in the front door.

Mrs. Racy, the breeder, laughed at Katy, who was hopping up and down with impatience as Mom and Dad followed her into the hall. "Come and see them," she said, leading everyone through to the sunroom. The door was blocked off with a board at knee height to keep the puppies in their own space. They were tumbling around all over the room, while their mother watched them from a comfortable cushion.

Katy couldn't see the little brown and white puppy she'd loved from the website. "There was one brown and white boy puppy in the photos. Is he gone already?" she asked anxiously.

Mrs. Racy looked around the room. "Oh, gosh, where did he go? He's the sneakiest of them all. Ah!" She pointed. "Look! See that big cardboard tube?"

Katy nodded. The tube was wriggling, and as she watched, a little brown nose appeared at one end, followed by some stubby whiskers and a pair of sparkling dark-brown eyes. The brown and white puppy popped out of the tube and stared curiously at the visitors.

"Oh, he's adorable!" Katy giggled.

"Do you want to go in and play with them?" Mrs. Racy asked.

"Yes, please!" Katy said eagerly.

"Are they okay with strangers?" Dad asked.

"They're very friendly," Mrs. Racy replied.

"Well, remember to be really gentle, Katy," said Dad.

Soon Katy's entire family was sitting on the floor, with puppies sniffing and licking and climbing over them. Even Diana couldn't resist the cuddly little things. There were only five puppies, but there seemed to be so many more as they all wriggled and darted around so quickly. The brown and white puppy was definitely in charge—or at least he thought he was. Katy watched him hopefully. She really wanted to pick him up, but she didn't want to scare him.

The puppy gave her an interested look. She smelled nice. Very friendly.

Katy gently held out the back of her hand for him to sniff, and he crept up to her, his tail wagging gently. He sniffed her fingers, then nudged them lovingly with his nose.

"Your nose is cold," Katy whispered. She ran her fingers over his silky, domed head. His fur was so soft.

The puppy closed his eyes blissfully and rested his chin on Katy's knee. That was *very* nice.

"He's a handsome little guy," Dad said. "What do you think, Katy? Is this the one?"

## Chapter Four
# The Reunion

There was a lot to do before Katy and her family could bring the puppy home. Katy, Diana, and their mom went to the pet store on the way home from school the next day with a long list. Katy had brought all her allowance money with her, although she didn't have much left after buying Christmas presents. It certainly wasn't enough to buy everything she wanted to get for their new puppy.

"Katy! Come and choose a collar and leash," Mom called from the counter. Katy left choosing between a squeaky fish and a bright-orange nylon bone and ran over.

"What color do you think?" Mom said thoughtfully. "This blue one is nice."

Katy nodded. "Yes…. But don't you think he'd look handsome with a red collar? It would show up really well against his brown and white fur." She lifted the bright collar and held it up.

Mom added the red collar and leash to the pile on the counter—a sleeping cushion, a big bag of puppy food, and food and water bowls. "Did you find a toy for him, Katy? And where's Diana? Did she want to get anything?"

"She's choosing a Christmas present for Misty. I'll get her. And I've almost decided which toys."

Katy managed to limit herself to three dog toys, and five minutes later they were walking home, laden down with bags.

"There's one thing missing, girls. We still need to decide what we're going to name the puppy. Ow, this food is heavy!" Mom shifted the bag to her other hand.

"I've been thinking about it!" Katy hitched up the big purple cushion they'd chosen for the puppy to sleep on. The man in the store had said some puppies liked to chew baskets, so cushions were better. "I think he really looks like a

Teddy. Sort of mischievous but cute."
She looked anxiously at Mom and Diana.

"Teddy…. I like it," Mom said.

Diana just shrugged. Even though she'd enjoyed cuddling the puppies at Mrs. Racy's house, she still wasn't sure that they should actually get one. "It's okay," she muttered.

Back at home, Katy wandered around the kitchen, trying out the cushion and bowls in different positions.

"Katy, I'm not cooking with a dog cushion in front of the oven," Mom pointed out. "Try by the radiator; that'll be nice and warm."

Katy pushed Misty's blanket out of the way and stood back to look at the cushion. "That's perfect!" she declared happily.

Misty prowled in from the hallway and stopped. Someone had put a big purple cushion exactly in her favorite sleeping spot. She stalked over and stared up at Katy accusingly.

"Hi, Misty!" Katy bent down to pet her. "Look, this is where your new friend is going to sleep. He's a puppy, and his name is Teddy. He's so sweet, and I bet you'll love him!"

Misty climbed onto her fleecy pink blanket and sat down, squishing herself in beside the huge cushion. She glared at it disapprovingly. What was going on?

Katy didn't notice. She was looking at the calendar on the wall and wishing it wasn't so long until they brought Teddy home. "Another three whole days until Saturday!" she sighed. "That's so long!"

The brown and white puppy gazed thoughtfully up at the window. It was only very slightly open, but the most delicious smells kept floating through it. Fresh air and frosty ground and general outside smells. It smelled *wonderful.* The puppies weren't allowed outside yet, since they were too young, but the brown and white puppy was desperate to explore. Where were all those delicious smells coming from?

He looked around. His brothers and sisters were snoozing in their basket, and their mother was half-asleep, too. If he went for a little walk now, probably nobody would notice....

Mrs. Racy had left the window open

to air out the room, but she'd carefully made sure it was only open a crack. Not that the puppies were big or strong enough to get up onto the windowsill, of course! They were much too small for that.

The puppy looked up. Beneath the window was a chair. It was still too high for him to reach, but next to that was the old cardboard box that Mrs. Racy had given them to play with. If he climbed onto that first, maybe he could jump onto the chair, and then to the window?

He scrambled onto the box, tiny claws scratching. Then he made the next hop onto the chair. Hmmm. It was still a long way to the windowsill. But....

"Oh, you naughty little thing!"

Mrs. Racy was half-laughing, half-angry, as she rescued the brown and white puppy, who was standing on the chair seat, his paws on the back, staring up at the open window hopefully. "You could have really hurt yourself. And I suppose you were trying to get to the window. I'd better shut that." She smiled. "I think your new family should call you Rascal. You're going to be a real handful!"

On Saturday morning, Katy woke up early with a wonderful feeling of excitement inside. She was still sleepy, and it took her a couple of minutes to figure out why she was feeling so happy. It was the first day of Christmas vacation, but there was something more…. Then she remembered. They were getting Teddy today! She bounced out of bed and flung on her clothes.

She clattered downstairs, wondering where everyone else was. Misty stared at her, annoyed, as she banged the kitchen door open, then turned around on her blanket and settled herself down with her back to Katy.

Katy was aching with impatience by the time the rest of the family got up. She couldn't understand how Dad could sit there with the paper and drink a cup of coffee so slowly.

"When are we going to *go*?" she wailed, standing in the doorway with her coat on.

"It only takes 20 minutes to get there in the car," Mom pointed out.

Katy frowned. "But it takes at least five minutes to get in the car! It's rude to be late, Mom. You're always saying that."

"Well, that still leaves us half an hour." Dad folded up the paper. "Anyone else want more toast?"

"OH!" Katy groaned and stomped out of the room.

At Mrs. Racy's house, the puppies were playing a fun game with  the big cardboard tube. It was just wide enough for them to get inside now, and they were scrambling through it, nipping at each other's tails.

Suddenly, there was a scratching, scuffling noise from inside the tube as the brown and white puppy shot out of one end. He shook his ears, then trotted hopefully over to Mrs. Racy. "What is it, boy? Oh, there's the doorbell." She smiled down at the puppy. "Did you hear the car? Someone special is coming for you!"

When Mrs. Racy answered the door, Katy had to stop herself from dashing into the house and hugging the puppy—she was already thinking of him as Teddy. But she knew she shouldn't. He was only little, and he probably wouldn't remember who she was. She would have to be really calm and gentle. But it was so hard when she was this excited!

Katy walked into the living room, digging her nails into the palms of her hands. Would Teddy even remember her?

The puppies were all standing by the door, watching to see who was coming. Suddenly, there was a piercing squeak of a bark, and a small brown and white ball of fur hurled itself at the board across the door, scratching madly. Two little white paws clawed their way over the top, and Teddy flung himself over the board, heading for Katy as fast as he could. He knew that girl! She was the one who'd cuddled him!

"Oh my goodness!" Mrs. Racy exclaimed. "None of them has ever done that before." She hurried forward. "Is he all right?"

Teddy was shaking himself dazedly—it had been a long way down for such a small dog—but then he barked again and ran to Katy.

Katy knelt down and hugged him to her lovingly. "Oh, Teddy. You remembered me!"

## Chapter Five
# An Unfriendly Encounter

Mrs. Racy had given them a special box for carrying Teddy home. Katy was a little disappointed because she'd been looking forward to cuddling him in the car, but Mom said it might be dangerous if he wriggled out of her arms. He'd feel safer in the box.

Katy wasn't so sure. She hated hearing the snuffling, whimpering noises that

Teddy was making behind her seat. He didn't sound happy at all.

"So when we get home, we're going to let Teddy out into the kitchen, girls. That's the plan," Mom reminded them. "He needs to get used to the house slowly. Remember, he's only been used to staying in the puppy room. The entire house would be too overwhelming for him. And then we need to introduce him to Misty very carefully."

"Can I show him my bedroom?" Katy asked hopefully.

"I wouldn't just yet," Dad told her, as they turned onto their street. "For starters, the mess would probably scare him out of his mind...."

Katy grinned. That was true. Teddy could very easily get lost in there. As soon as the car stopped, she struggled out of her seat belt, her fingers clumsy with excitement, and gently lifted Teddy's box out of the back. She could feel him skidding around inside, even though she was walking so slowly and carefully. "We'll get you out in just a minute," she whispered. "You can see your new home!"

Katy carried Teddy into the house and put the box down on the kitchen floor, kneeling beside it. Then she undid the flaps that held it together. Teddy stared up at her, puzzled by his strange, dark journey. But then he recognized Katy and gave a pleased little whine, scratching at the cardboard with his claws to show her he wanted to get out.

"Come on, Teddy!" Katy lifted him

out and cuddled him lovingly. He was staring at her, his big, dark eyes bright and interested. Then all at once he reached up and licked Katy's chin, making her splutter and giggle.

"Well, I don't mind if you do that, but I wouldn't do it to Mom," she whispered to him.

Teddy gazed at her lovingly. He was a little confused about what was going on—his brothers and sisters weren't here, nor was his mom, but if he was going to get cuddled and played with, maybe it would be all right.

He wondered if there were any other dogs here. He couldn't smell them, but there was another smell, a different smell that he didn't recognize....

"How's he doing, Katy?" Dad had come in from the car. He and Mom and Diana had been chatting to the lady next door and telling her about their new arrival.

"I'm just about to show him his cushion and his food bowl," Katy explained. She walked around the kitchen with Teddy, holding him up to see out the back door. Then she put him gently down next to his cushion. "This is where you're going to sleep. Look."

Mom came in holding Teddy's collar and leash. "Don't forget these, Katy.

Remember what the website said—we need to keep him on the leash in case we have to stop him from chasing Misty."

"Oh, yes!" Katy bent down and fastened the bright-red collar around Teddy's neck. "Very handsome!" she said. She clipped on the leash, and Teddy looked at it in surprise. What was this? Oh, a leash, like his mom had.

He sniffed at the big purple cushion and sneezed.

Dad laughed. "It probably smells clean. Don't worry, Teddy; it'll be smelling like a dog in a couple of days."

Just then, Diana came in carrying Misty. She'd gone to get her from upstairs. Misty spent most of her time snoozing on Diana's bed.

Teddy was delighted. He peered up

at Misty, his whiskers twitching. So that was what the interesting smell he'd noticed was! A friend! He danced clumsily over to her on his too-big puppy paws and barked cheerfully to say hello. Katy followed, holding his leash and watching them cautiously.

The fur on Misty's back stood up on end, and her tail fluffed up to twice its normal size. She hissed warningly. *Stay away!*

"Teddy...," Katy said anxiously, but Teddy wasn't listening. He had no experience with cats, so he didn't recognize Misty's warning for what it was. He just wanted to say hello to this big, fluffy animal.

Misty hissed again, then yowled and spat, her ears flat against her head.

Teddy stared at her, feeling very confused. Then he backed up a little. He didn't understand what was going on, but he could tell now that something was wrong. He looked up at Katy and whimpered, asking for help.

"I told you she'd hate it!" Diana said

accusingly to Mom. "Oh, Misty, no!"
Misty had jumped out of her arms and
was prowling across the kitchen toward
Teddy.

Katy was just stooping to pick him
up when Misty pounced and swiped
her paw across Teddy's nose—not very
hard, just enough to make it clear she
really wanted him gone.

Teddy howled in surprise and
dismay. His nose did hurt, but it was
more the shock of it that upset him so
much. He'd played rough games with
his brothers and sisters, but no one had
ever scratched him before. He buried
his nose in Katy's sweater as she picked
him up, and snuffled miserably.

Misty hissed at him triumphantly,
her fur still bristling.

"That was so mean of Misty!" Katy cried angrily. "All he did was try to say hello, and she clawed him! His nose is bleeding!" She snuggled Teddy close and glared at Diana and Misty.

"Maybe we should put Teddy's cushion in the laundry room to start," Dad said worriedly, looking at Teddy's nose. "I think it's too much for Misty to get used to all at once."

Diana folded her arms and stared at the ceiling. "I told you this was a bad idea," she said. "Misty hates dogs, and this is her home. It's *never* going to work."

"Well, now it's Teddy's home, too!" Katy snapped back. "Misty is just going to have to get used to it!"

Katy sat up on her bed in the dark, her comforter wrapped around her shoulders, listening anxiously as

Teddy let out another mournful howl. Everyone had agreed that he would stay in the kitchen and the laundry room at first so he could get used to the house gradually. It was what all the dog books and websites had suggested, especially since Teddy was still learning to ask to go outside if he needed to. Mom really didn't want him messing up all the carpets.

Mom and Dad had been careful to keep Misty away from Teddy for the rest of the day after their fight. For tonight they'd put a litter box in the hall, and Misty was sleeping on Diana's bed, as she always did. Katy had begged her parents to let Teddy sleep in her room, too, just for his first night, but Mom had said definitely not.

Teddy just didn't understand why he couldn't explore the rest of the house. Katy had stayed in the kitchen almost all that day, playing with him, and cuddling him, but Teddy had still been curious about what was going on everywhere else.

That cat was allowed to go wherever she liked, but he had to stay in, except when he was taken into the yard to do his business. It didn't seem fair. And when she wanted to be in the kitchen to eat her food, he had to go into the laundry room! Why couldn't he eat with her? She might even have leftovers.

But the worst thing was that now they'd all gone to bed. He had to sleep in the kitchen, and he was all on his own! It was so lonely! Where was everyone?

He howled so much that Katy just couldn't get to sleep. She sat there listening to the sorrowful wails from downstairs, and eventually she couldn't stand it any longer. She crept out of bed, wrapping her comforter around her like a cloak and trailing it along behind her. Mom might have said Katy absolutely must not have Teddy in her room, but she hadn't said anything about not sleeping in the kitchen with Teddy, had she?

Teddy was sitting on his cushion, staring anxiously into the darkness. Like all dogs, he could see well in the dark, but he wasn't used to being all alone— he never had been before. What if Katy never came back? He didn't want to be on his own forever! Teddy whimpered again, and then stopped. He could hear footsteps, and an odd swishing noise. What was that?

He looked worriedly at the door, hoping it wasn't something horrible. Maybe the cat was coming to be mean to him again. In his mind, she was about twice her real size, and her tail was enormous. Maybe that was what the strange noise was…. Teddy whined nervously.

Katy hitched up her trailing comforter and gently pushed the door open. She called softly to him. "Teddy? Hey, sweetie!"

Teddy heaved a huge sigh of relief and trotted over to her.

"Oops!" Katy giggled. "I just walked into a chair! It's so dark."

Teddy woofed in agreement. Dark, and lonely. He gazed hopefully up at her.

"Look, I brought my comforter. I've come to keep you company for a while. You're used to having your mom to sleep with, aren't you?" Katy curled up next to Teddy's cushion, and he snuggled gratefully onto her lap. This was much better.

Katy smiled down at him as he dozed off into a deep puppy sleep. He was hers, at last! The kitchen floor was cold on her toes, but she didn't care. It was worth it.

## Chapter Six
# A Grumpy Cat

Katy's mom came downstairs on Sunday morning and found them both curled up together, Katy with her head on Teddy's cushion, and him snuggled under the comforter with her.

"Katy! I thought you were still in bed! Actually, I was surprised you weren't up and playing with Teddy already." Mom sighed as she poured Katy some juice and filled Teddy's food bowl. "I should have known."

Katy grinned. "Sorry, Mom. He was so lonely. I listened to him whining and crying forever, and then I just couldn't stand it any longer."

"The thing is, now he'll expect you to do it again tonight." Mom watched as Teddy wolfed down his breakfast. "You can't sleep on the kitchen floor every night, Katy!"

Katy wriggled her shoulders. "I know. This floor's really hard. Honestly, Mom, I won't do it again. I think he was just miserable the first night, that's all."

Katy was right. Teddy had never been left alone before, and he hadn't been sure that anyone would ever come back for him. Now that he knew that Katy and the rest of the family weren't far away, and he'd see them in the morning, he didn't mind being alone so much.

In fact, on Sunday night, he was so worn out from playing in the yard with Katy for most of the day that he curled up on his cushion and fell asleep almost as soon as she went to bed. He didn't bother with even one little howl.

A couple of days later, Katy's parents decided that Teddy had settled in so well that they could let him explore a little further.

"Just downstairs, though," Dad said. "There's so much stuff he could accidentally damage upstairs. Imagine if he started chewing your mom's shoe collection. She'd never forgive him!"

Katy nodded, although she wished she could have Teddy in her room. Still, she was really looking forward to curling up with him to watch TV in the living room.

"Come on, Teddy," she called, standing by the kitchen door and patting her knees. "Come on, boy!"

Teddy looked at her with his head to one side. He wasn't quite sure what was happening. He wasn't allowed out of that door, was he? He'd been told no when he tried before. He padded slowly over to Katy, then turned and looked at her mom, waiting to see if she'd scold him.

Mom laughed. "It's okay, Teddy. Go on, go with Katy."

Teddy woofed with excitement and trotted happily into the hallway. New things to smell! He worked his way curiously along Katy and Diana's school bags and boots, which were by the front door, then poked his nose into the living room. Diana was sitting on the couch reading a magazine, with Misty on her lap.

Over the last couple of days, Katy and Diana and Mom and Dad had very carefully kept Teddy and Misty apart. They wanted to give Teddy time to settle down, and Misty needed to get used to the idea of a dog in the house.

Misty spent as much time as she possibly could in Diana's room, only coming into the kitchen to gobble up her food—with one watchful eye on the laundry room door the entire time. She would then shoot out of the cat flap and rely on Diana letting her in the front door when she wanted to come in again. Now she looked up at Teddy and hissed.

"Oh, Misty!" Katy sighed. "Don't be so grumpy."

Teddy had almost forgotten his first meeting with the cat. He was still little, and he was naturally friendly. He assumed everyone else was, too. He bounced over toward Misty and Diana, his tail wagging, and yapped excitedly at her. Misty shot onto the arm of the couch and growled, her back arching.

Teddy's tail drooped, and he looked

at Katy. He was only trying to be friendly. *Why doesn't she like me?*

"Keep him away from Misty," Diana said irritably. "He's upsetting her."

"Mom said we could watch TV," Katy said. "There's a safari program on; I thought Teddy could watch it with me. Anyway, Misty and Teddy have to learn to get along. If we can just get them used to being in the same room, that would be really good."

"I suppose…," Diana muttered. "Just keep an eye on him, though!"

For the next half-hour, Misty glowered from the arm of the couch, her tail twitching warningly, and Teddy shot her curious, sidelong glances from the armchair, where he was curled up on Katy's lap.

Gradually, Misty started to relax, and after a while she dozed off on the arm of the couch, with one eye half-open.

Teddy sat quietly for a while, but soon

he began to feel restless. He slipped down from Katy's knee and went exploring. This was much more exciting! Katy was half-watching him, but the little lion cubs on the program were so cute!

Teddy sniffed his way around the room, investigating behind the Christmas tree and sneezing at the dust under the big bookcase. He even managed to wriggle under the couch. It was dark, and it smelled interesting. He could pop his head out from underneath, too, and then hide again, which made Katy giggle. It was a good game.

He crawled the entire length of the couch, and poked his nose out at Diana's end. There was an interesting fluffy thing there, dangling down, and twitching gently.

Teddy was mesmerized. It went back and forth, waving at him. The fluffy thing was like one of the toys Katy had given him, a furry rat that squeaked. Maybe this one would squeak, too, if he bit it…. He wriggled a little further out from under the couch, just as Katy realized she hadn't seen him for a minute or so.

"Where's Teddy? Is he behind the couch? Oh, Teddy, no!"

And Teddy pounced on Misty's tail….

## Chapter Seven
# Disturbing the Peace

Misty shot up in the air with a screech, and Teddy howled in shock—he hadn't expected the fluffy toy to do *that*…. He peeked nervously from under the couch just as Misty raced out of the room. Why was she so upset? Maybe it was *her* fluffy toy.

"Oh, Teddy…," Katy said worriedly. She was trying to sound angry, but she couldn't help smiling a tiny smile—Misty had looked so funny, like something out of a cartoon, as she'd leaped into the air.

"I'm telling Mom!" Diana snapped. "He did that on purpose, and you weren't watching him!" Then she ran after Misty.

Katy picked Teddy up. "Oh, Teddy. That was her tail. I don't think you knew that, though, did you? You didn't do it on purpose. I know you didn't. Our plan to get you and Misty to like each other isn't going very well, is it…."

And things got worse and worse over the next week. Rather than Misty and Teddy getting used to each other as time went on, Misty just got more and more furious about her peaceful home being invaded. She tried as hard as she could to stay away from Teddy, but she couldn't escape from him. It seemed that wherever she went, there he was, too.

Teddy didn't understand that Misty wanted to be left alone. She kept running off upstairs whenever he tried to play with her, and when he tried to follow he got scolded.

He was allowed out on his own in the yard now, though, and he thought he'd had a stroke of luck one afternoon when he found her snoozing on the bench in a patch of winter sunlight— she couldn't dash away up the stairs now! But she raced up to the top of the apple tree and snarled at him while he barked hopefully. But eventually, he gave up and ran over to Katy, who was calling him in.

Back in the kitchen, Teddy lay quietly on Katy's lap, even though she bounced his squeaky ball for him. His ears were drooping, and he rested his nose on his paws, gazing sadly at the back door.

"You really want her to play with you, don't you?" Katy sighed. "I think Misty's a little too old for playing, Teddy."

Teddy heard the worry in her voice and rubbed his head against her arm lovingly.

But Katy was right. Misty was an old cat, and stubborn. She didn't like new things, and she found it so strange and upsetting having Teddy around that

she didn't even want to eat anymore.
Besides, her food was in the kitchen,
where he was. It was easier just not to
bother. As the days went by, she started
to look thinner.

A few days before Christmas,
Teddy was curled up on his cushion,
feeling bored. Katy had left him in
the kitchen, explaining that she had to
go upstairs and wrap presents in her
room, because they were a secret, and
no one was supposed to see. Teddy
still wasn't allowed upstairs, but she
promised she'd be back soon.

Katy had shut the kitchen door when
she went upstairs, but Teddy had been
practicing, and he could claw it open
unless it was shut really tight. Teddy
hooked his claws into the crack and

scratched until it clicked open. Then he trotted cheerfully out. He was so clever! Katy had been gone for a long time. He was sure she wouldn't mind if he went to find her, would she?

Teddy headed for the stairs and suddenly felt a little less clever. They were very big. He almost couldn't see the top. But he knew Katy would be up there. He could smell her, and as a tracking dog, his sense of smell was excellent.

He heaved himself

up onto the first step, which wasn't too difficult, except that there were a lot more of them before he got to the top. Teddy sighed and looked up at the next step. It took him 10 minutes to get all the way up, and he almost went back to his comfy cushion several times.

But the exciting new smells upstairs soon made him forget how hard it had been to get there, and he set off snuffling along the carpet. Ah! An open door! Maybe Katy was here. No, it didn't smell like Katy. But there was Misty, curled up asleep on the purple comforter. Teddy trotted eagerly into the room. He was so excited to see her. If he woke her, maybe she would play with him. He stood up with his front paws on the edge of the bed and licked

Misty's nose. He could barely reach.

Misty was sleeping peacefully, knowing *that dog* was downstairs and she didn't need to worry. Then she woke up with a sudden fright.

He was right there! There, in Diana's room! Was nowhere safe anymore? Misty leaped off the bed and raced across the room, looking for a way to escape. Teddy was whining, trying to show her he was friendly, but all Misty could see was Teddy in the one place she'd felt was safe. Desperately she clawed her way up Diana's curtains and onto the top of the wardrobe.

The scuffling and barking brought Diana running upstairs; Katy rushed in after her.

"He's not supposed to be in here!"

Diana yelled. "Get him out of my room! Misty, it's okay, come on down, kitty, kitty…." She turned back to Katy, who was standing by the door, looking horrified. "Go on, get him out!" she cried angrily.

Teddy flinched back. Diana was so angry with him, and Misty was cowering on top of the wardrobe…. It had all gone wrong! He'd only been trying to be friendly. And now he was in trouble again!

Katy scooped him up and hurried downstairs. "Oh, Teddy! You shouldn't chase Misty! It's mean!"

*Katy sounds angry*, Teddy thought miserably. He sighed. He hadn't meant to be naughty.

"What's going on up there?" Mom

**85**

was standing at the bottom of the stairs looking worried.

"Katy let Teddy get into my room, and now Misty's stuck on top of my wardrobe!" Diana yelled from upstairs. "Mom, we have to shut him in the kitchen so Misty can calm down. It's just not fair."

"Oh, Katy. Did he upset Misty again?"

Teddy whined sadly as he heard another angry voice.

"Diana is right, Katy," Mom said firmly. "Put Teddy back in the kitchen, and make sure the door's shut tight. And hurry, Katy, we've got to finish the Christmas shopping this morning, remember. We need to get going."

"But Mom, he doesn't really like being shut in...," Katy started to say, but Mom gave her a stern look, folding her arms. Katy sighed. "Sorry, Teddy. You have to go back in the kitchen. Stay here and be good, all right?"

Teddy watched, his big, dark eyes mournful, as she carefully shut the door. He was all alone, and everybody was angry with him. He howled miserably at the ceiling, then slumped on his cushion, listening to Katy and Diana and Mom in the hallway, getting ready to go out.

Teddy wriggled around sadly, trying to get comfortable. A piece of pink material was hanging on the radiator, and he knocked it down as he turned. It made him jump as it fell onto his cushion. Teddy took it in his mouth to pull it out of the way, but he had it tangled in

his paws, and it tore a
little. This was
fun....

The pink
fabric was
good to
chew. It made
satisfying tearing noises as he shredded
it and shook it and rolled around the
floor with it. He felt much better
afterward, but very tired. It had been a
busy morning climbing all those stairs.

Teddy fell asleep, covered in small
pieces of pink fleece.

A couple of hours later, Katy, Mom,
and Diana came back. Teddy could

hear them outside the kitchen, and he  scratched the door a few times hopefully, but no one came to get him. He could hear Diana talking to Misty. *She* was allowed out. It wasn't fair. He trailed back to his cushion and nibbled some more pink fleece.

"Where's Misty's blanket, Mom?" Diana called. "It's not in my room, and you know she likes to sleep on it."

"Oh, I washed it, Diana. It was so dirty. It's hanging on the kitchen radiator to dry," Mom said.

Teddy could hear Diana coming toward the door, whispering to Misty. "It's all right. We'll get your blanket, then you can have a nice nap."

As Diana opened the kitchen door, cuddling Misty, a guilty-looking brown and white puppy stared up at her, with shreds of pink blanket hanging out of the corner of his mouth.

## Chapter Eight
# The Lost Cat

Teddy lay on his cushion silently, only occasionally giving a sad little whine. Diana had been so angry, angrier than anyone had ever been with him. She'd called him a bad dog, and a lot of other horrible things. Even *Katy* had said he was naughty. He'd never heard her sound upset like that. And the worst thing was, they were right. He *had* been naughty.

The kitchen door clicked open gently, and Katy came in wearing her pajamas. Teddy looked up at her sadly. Was she still angry with him?

"Oh, Teddy. I'm sorry we shouted. You didn't know, did you? But Misty's really upset, Teddy, and Diana is *furious*." Katy sighed. "I thought you and Misty would learn to get along, but it just isn't happening." She petted his ears gently, and Teddy laid his nose on her knee, gazing apologetically at her.

Katy looked guiltily around at the kitchen door, and then scooped him up in her arms. "Come on. We're both too miserable to be on our own. Mom and Dad have gone to bed, so I'm going to sneak you up to my room. We've got to be really quiet, because if anyone catches us, we'll be in big trouble, okay?"

Teddy snuggled gratefully into Katy's arms, and she tiptoed upstairs. She tucked him down beside her, and Teddy felt happy for the first time since Diana had been so angry. At least Katy still loved him.

But the next morning, Diana flung Katy's bedroom door open and rushed in, her face panicky.

Katy rolled over. "What is it?" she asked, too sleepy to remember that she should hide Teddy. Luckily, Diana seemed too distracted to notice him.

"Have you seen Misty?" she asked anxiously.

Katy shook her head, yawning.

"She didn't come back in last night! I was sure she'd be here this morning. She does stay out late sometimes, but never all night." She frowned at Katy. "You know why she's gone, don't you? Because of Teddy. He's driven her away, Katy!"

"That's not true—" Katy started to say, but Diana didn't let her finish.

"Of course it is! He eats her food, he chases her, he's bitten her tail, and now he's chewed up her most special thing! I'm just surprised she didn't leave before!"

Katy sat up in bed, carefully covering Teddy with the comforter. "Misty's just old and grumpy, and she's never been friendly to Teddy. She was the one who

**94**

scratched him!"

"She's a cat, Katy! Cats don't like dogs! I told you and Mom and Dad that, and nobody listened, and now we've lost her. You were the one who wanted a dog in the first place. It's all your fault!"

"No, it isn't!" Katy yelled back, making Teddy tremble beside her. He hated shouting.

"It is, and stop trying to hide Teddy, because I know you've got him up here, and I'm telling Mom!" Diana stormed out, leaving Teddy whimpering.

"It's okay, boy," Katy muttered. "It'll be okay...."

But she wasn't at all sure that it would.

Katy and Teddy were miserable. Diana was still claiming that Misty had run away because of Teddy. Katy had to admit it was true, but he hadn't been naughty on purpose—he was just being a dog, a friendly, bouncy puppy. He hadn't meant to upset Misty!

Dad had called their vet to tell them that Misty was missing. Misty had been microchipped, so that if anyone brought her into the vet, they could tell at once who she belonged to. But Mom and Dad were sure that she would be back soon.

"It's only been one night, Diana," Mom said at breakfast, putting an arm around her.

Katy sat on the other side of the table, feeling miserable. She was worried about Misty, too, and Mom had really scolded her for having Teddy in her room. Now he was lying under the table, resting his nose on her feet. He could sense how upset everyone was, and it was horrible.

"She'll be back as soon as she gets hungry, Diana," Dad promised. "And it's the first morning of my vacation from work, remember, so I can help you look for her later if she doesn't turn up."

"It's only two days until Christmas!" Diana wailed. "What if Misty isn't back for Christmas Day?"

The problem was that Misty didn't want to be found. She was miserable, and she wanted to hide from people, and especially from *dogs*. When she had seen her precious blanket in pieces all over the kitchen floor, she had known that she couldn't stay in the house any longer.

Misty had left home, and she wasn't coming back. Not while the dog was still there. She had plodded dismally through the yard, crawled under the back fence, and set off down the alley that led to the main street. She wanted to be far away, and by the time Diana had finished shouting at Katy and Teddy and raced after her, Misty had gone too far to hear her frantic calling.

Misty liked being outdoors. She was good at hunting—she loved to give Diana mice as presents—and she loved lying in the sun in the yard. Only now it was freezing, and she could smell snow in the air. And it felt different being outside all alone and knowing that she couldn't just slip back in through her cat flap to be safe and warm again.

She spent the night huddled next to a shed a few streets away from her own house. It was horrible; still, she couldn't go back. But when she woke in the morning, hungry and stiff with cold, Misty wished that Diana was there to cuddle her and open one of her favorite cans of fish-flavored food for breakfast. Maybe she should go home, just to eat, and then she could leave again, after she'd seen Diana....

Misty crawled out of the grubby little den she'd found and sniffed the air anxiously. Home was—which way?

In a sudden panic, Misty leaped onto the top of a wall, looking worriedly around. She didn't know! She had been so desperate to get away yesterday that she hadn't tried to remember. Now all the yards looked the same, and none of them was hers....

## Chapter Nine
# A Christmas to Remember

It was the saddest Christmas Day ever. The entire family was sitting in the living room, with the Christmas tree lights on, trying to be enthusiastic about presents. Carols were playing, and it looked like a perfect Christmas scene. Even Teddy had a ribbon around his collar. But there was a cat-shaped hole where Misty should have been perched on the back of the sofa, waiting to pounce on the crackly wrapping paper. Everyone was thinking about her.

"Your turn, Diana!" Mom said brightly.

Diana stared at the pile of gifts in front of her as though she wasn't really seeing them. She was holding a plastic packet in her hands, with a picture on it that looked very much like Misty. Katy looked over at her miserably. She'd been with Diana at the pet store when she'd bought it—the luxury cat "chocolates" that were meant to have been Misty's Christmas present.

Tears started to seep out of the corners of Diana's eyes, and Mom sighed. "Let's leave the rest of the presents until later."

Dad stood up. "Come on, Katy—

it's time for Teddy's big Christmas present!"

Katy nodded. She and Dad had planned a long time ago to take Teddy for his first walk on Christmas Day. Katy had been looking forward to it ever since they got Teddy—they'd had to wait until he'd had all of his vaccinations before he could go out and meet other dogs. They were going to take him just as far as the park near Katy and Diana's school so he wouldn't get too tired out. "Teddy, walk! Come on!"

Teddy raced to the front door, leaping excitedly around Katy's legs, squeaking and whining with delight. They were going out! Katy had his leash. He'd seen other dogs at his old house with them on, and he knew it meant a walk.

"Teddy, calm down! Shh! Look, if you don't keep still, I won't even be able to get it on you!" Katy was half-laughing, half-annoyed. She was trying to clip the leash to Teddy's collar, but he kept licking her hand and barking, and then rushing to scratch at the door.

Katy's dad grabbed his coat and stuffed a handful of papers into his pocket.

"What are those?" Katy asked.

Her dad sighed. "Just some more posters. I promised Diana."

"Oh…." Katy nodded. Suddenly, the excitement about their first walk faded a little. Diana had papered their neighborhood with "lost" posters during the last couple of days, but no one had called to say they'd seen a fluffy gray cat.

Katy wondered if she should go and ask Diana if she should take some, too, but Diana still wasn't speaking to her.

Teddy looked up at them and whined again. He felt the change in Katy, that suddenly she wasn't happy anymore. He guessed it was because of Misty— everyone was unhappy about her. He missed her, too, even though she would never play with him. He hung his head sadly.

Diana wandered into the hallway, followed by Mom, who was looking at her watch. "I need to get the food ready for dinner. You go with them, Diana. You can't sit around all day. I know you don't want to, but honestly, getting some fresh air will make you feel better."

"Oh, Mom, no…," Diana muttered.

"I mean it, Diana. Go and get your coat on." Mom gave Diana a quick hug and a gentle push in the direction of the door. "Go!"

Even Diana trailing along in a miserable cloud couldn't stop Teddy from dancing around and winding his leash around Katy's legs as they headed out the front door. There was so much to see, so many delicious new smells. He was sure there must be at least a hundred other dogs on this street—he could smell them all! Teddy suddenly stopped, almost tripping Katy up with his leash.

"I think Teddy might need some obedience classes soon," Dad said, laughing.

Katy tried to coax him to move, but Teddy wasn't listening. He'd had a great idea. He could smell all those dogs so clearly. He was good at smelling things. So maybe he could sniff out Misty! He bounded ahead, his nose busily at work. There were a lot of cat smells, too….

Misty was hiding behind a big, smelly garbage can in a tiny yard behind a row of stores on the way to Katy and Diana's school.

It was awful. There were rats, and although Misty liked to hunt mice, the rats were not the same thing at all. They were big and frightening. She was huddled inside a tattered cardboard box, and every so often a rat would scurry past. The only good thing about the yard was that there was a lot of food around, although it wasn't as nice as those special cans of food that

Diana gave her.

Diana…. Misty got up and turned around anxiously. She didn't want to think about Diana. She missed Diana so much, but Diana didn't care about her anymore. Diana had let a dog into the house. Even into Misty and Diana's room. That wasn't Misty's home now. Diana didn't love her anymore.

But what was she going to do? Another rat scuttled past, baring its teeth at Misty. She couldn't stay here, but she had no idea where to go. *I need a new home*, Misty thought miserably. *But I don't want one. I want my old home back!*

*And I'd even share it with that dog if it meant I could still be with Diana….*

Teddy was the only one enjoying the walk. He danced around, sniffing and scratching happily as they reached the stores and all those interesting smells. There were definitely cats here, too.

Diana was silent, trudging along with her head down—except when they happened to see a cat, when she'd look up hopefully, then sigh and stare at the pavement again.

"I think it's going to snow." Dad was looking up at the sky. "The clouds have that grayish look. And it's certainly cold enough. I'm freezing. Should we turn back, girls?"

"Mmm. Come on, Teddy." Katy tugged gently on his leash. But Teddy wasn't listening. He was straining forward against the leash, looking

**111**

excited. Then he turned and gazed anxiously at Katy and uttered a sharp, urgent bark.

*Can you smell what I smell?*

"Teddy, we're going home. Come on, boy."

*No! Not now! We have to go this way!*

"Ted-dy!" Katy's voice was starting to sound angry.

Teddy looked worriedly up at her. How could he make her understand? He had a terrible feeling that she wasn't going to. But he was sure he recognized that smell and he had to investigate…. Teddy gave Katy an apologetic look with his big, dark eyes and moved a step toward her, loosening his leash.

"Good boy, Teddy," Katy said in a relieved voice.

Then Teddy jumped back suddenly, dragging his leash out of Katy's hand, and dashed down a little alley, following that familiar scent. Now where was it coming from?

Katy stared down at her hand for a second, as though expecting the leash still to be in it. Then she raced after Teddy, calling anxiously to him.

"Katy! Teddy!" Dad had been staring at the snow clouds and looked back just in time to see Katy vanishing down the alley, too.

Teddy bounded into the little yard, trailing his leash, and stopped, looking around. Now that he was here, there were a lot of other smells, too—old food, and strange animal smells that he wasn't too sure about. But yes…. There was a definite hint of Misty's scent, too. She was this way. He trotted over to the garbage cans, poking his nose between them hopefully. Yes! There she was! Curled up in an old cardboard box, and staring fearfully back at him.

Teddy barked for joy. He'd found her! He called excitedly for Katy to come, and then rushed at Misty. He was just so glad to see her. Now everyone would be happy! He licked Misty's nose, and she shuddered and hissed, backing further into the box. Teddy stepped back doubtfully. *Aren't you happy to see me?*

Misty gave a sad little meow. Where was Diana? Maybe the dog could show her? She edged slowly out of the box, the fur on her spine slightly raised. *Don't lick me again*, she was telling Teddy. *But I'm not angry. Yet.*

Katy skidded into the yard, calling anxiously. "Teddy! Teddy, where are you?" She spotted his red leash,

**115**

trailing out between the garbage cans. "Oh, Teddy, are you eating something awful?" She ran over, squeezing herself between the garbage cans, and Teddy stared up at her proudly.

*Look! I've found her!* he barked.

"What is it?" Katy asked, peering a little reluctantly into the box. She had a horrible feeling Teddy had found something yucky. "Misty! Oh, Misty!" Katy whirled around. "Diana, Diana, come here, quick!"

Diana and Dad were just following them up the alley. "You've caught him!" cried Dad. "Thank goodness."

"Yes, but look!" Katy picked Teddy up and hugged him lovingly. "Diana, come and see!" She stood back so Diana could get to the box. "Teddy's found her. He must have sniffed her out. That's why he ran off. He's so clever."

Diana dropped to her knees beside the box. "Misty!" she whispered.

Misty shot out of the box and Diana swooped down and picked her up. Misty snuggled into Diana's coat, purring so hard her sides were shuddering.

"Katy, he found her!" Cradling Misty in her arms, Diana turned to her sister and Teddy. "I can't believe it…."

Teddy reached out from Katy's arms, wriggling and wagging his tail happily, and amazingly, Misty didn't snarl or hiss at him. She shut her eyes slightly as he licked her nose. She didn't look like she was enjoying it, but she let him.

"They're friends!" Katy said in amazement.

Misty glared at her, as if to say, *Don't push it….*

But it was true. And above them, the first Christmas snowflakes were starting to float gently down.

"Misty, Teddy, turkey!" Katy laughed at Misty and Teddy, both standing eagerly by their food bowls. "Just a little. It's your Christmas dinner."

"Get going and eat yours, Katy,"

Mom said. "Dad is almost finished."

"Don't worry. I'll be having seconds," Dad said with his mouth full.

Diana wasn't eating very much, either. Both girls just kept stopping and staring happily at Misty and Teddy, who were wolfing down turkey.

"I hope Misty likes her new blanket," Katy said, ignoring the roast potato that she was waving around.

"I bet she will. Look, she's about to try it out. It's a beautiful present, Katy." Diana smiled at her, and Katy grinned back. It felt like the first time in weeks that Diana had smiled so easily at her. The angry wall between them seemed to have just crumbled away.

Misty prowled thoughtfully over to the new pink, fleecy blanket that lay neatly by the heater. Katy had bought it weeks ago on a trip to the pet store. She'd seen how old and tattered Misty's blanket had become and had decided it was the perfect Christmas present.

Misty walked around it a couple of times, then graciously stepped onto it, testing it with her paws. She lay down, the picture of a comfy, turkey-fed cat, and purred.

Teddy finished licking the last possible taste of turkey out of his bowl and gave Misty's bowl a quick lick just in case she'd left any. He sighed happily. Then he trotted over to Misty's blanket and gazed hopefully at her.

Misty gave him a resigned look. *If you must*, she seemed to be saying.

Katy and Diana watched, holding their breath, as Teddy whined eagerly and snuggled down next to Misty, putting his nose next to hers.

Misty put a firm paw on one of his long, curly brown ears. Clearly, if Teddy was on her blanket, he had to keep still.

Teddy looked up at Katy lovingly and yawned. Two minutes later, both cat and puppy were fast asleep.

Diana put her arm around Katy's shoulder, and Katy smiled. It was a perfect Christmas after all.

Available now:

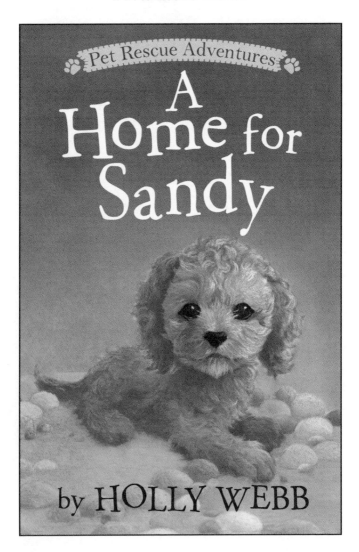

Pet Rescue Adventures

A Home for Sandy

by HOLLY WEBB

Available now:

Pet Rescue Adventures

Lost in the Storm

by HOLLY WEBB

## HOLLY WEBB

Holly Webb started out as a children's book editor, and wrote her first series for the publisher she worked for. She has been writing ever since, with more than 100 books to her name. Holly lives in England with her husband, three young sons, and several cats who are always nosing around when she is trying to type on her laptop.

For more information
about Holly Webb visit:

# www.holly-webb.com
www.tigertalesbooks.com